THE LEGEND OF ST. GEORGE

A Thrilling Crime Mystery

ARIEL SANDERS

Copyright © 2025 by ARIEL SANDERS
All rights reserved.

No part of this book may be reproduced, stored in a retrieval system, or transmitted in any form or by any means—electronic, mechanical, photocopying, recording, or otherwise—without the prior written permission of the publisher, except in the case of brief quotations used in reviews.

This book is intended for entertainment purposes only. While every effort has been made to ensure accuracy, the author and publisher make no representations or warranties regarding the completeness, accuracy, or reliability of the information contained within. The reader assumes full responsibility for their interpretation and application of any content in this book.

Index

Prologue The Cursed Land   5
Chapter 1 The Knight Without a Cause   9
Chapter 2 The Chosen One   17
Chapter 3 The Hunter's Path   29
Epilogue The River of Stars   45

SPECIAL BONUS

Want this Bonus Ebook for *free*?

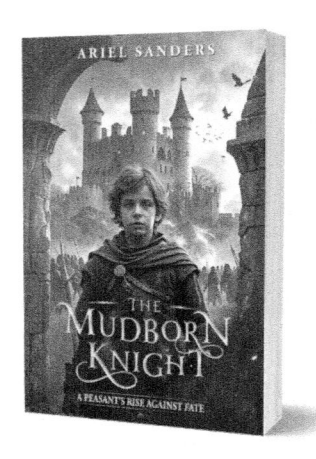

SCAN W/ YOUR CAMERA TO DOWNLOAD THE EBOOK!

SCAN ME

Prologue
The Cursed Land

Rain fell over Silene, dark and thick. Not water, but something else—something that stained the cobblestones and left rusty streaks on window glass. The townsfolk called it the dragon's tears, though tears implied sorrow, and whatever lurked beyond the Blightwood felt nothing so human.

Elias Thorne trudged through the narrow streets, his hood pulled low against the downpour. The wetness seeped through the wool, ran down his neck, smelled of copper and rot. He kept his eyes on the uneven stones before him, avoiding puddles that reflected nothing, not even moonlight.

Silene had once been called the jewel of the eastern kingdoms. Its fields yielded twice the grain of neighboring lands. Its orchards drooped heavy with fruit. The rivers teemed with fish that leapt into waiting nets. Children grew strong, winters passed quickly, and the city's markets overflowed with silk and spice from far-off lands.

That was before.

Before the ground turned sulfurous. Before livestock dropped stillborn. Before the dreams began—terrible visions that woke sleepers screaming, visions they couldn't speak of without their tongues cleaving to the roof of their mouths.

Before the dragon.

A dragon as the old tales described—a scaled beast belching fire, a winged terror. But this was something worse than even the legends warned of. This dragon was ancient, massive, its scales the color of dried blood, its eyes burning with malevolence that scorched the mind of any who dared to look upon it directly. Its mere presence had strangled the land like a vine choking an oak.

No one alive remembered when it came. The oldest records spoke of a night centuries ago when the moon burned blood-red, when the earth groaned, when a fissure split the ancient temple at the forest's heart. From that fissure emerged the beast, its wings casting shadows that killed crops in an instant, its roar shattering glass for miles.

That night, every child in Silene woke screaming from the same nightmare. Every pregnant woman lost her unborn. Every elder closed their eyes and never opened them again.

Then came the emissary, a figure of shadow wearing robes of indigo and gold. It spoke with many voices layered atop one another, like a chorus of the damned. The dragon would spare the kingdom, it said. The dragon would permit life to continue. But there would be a price.

One maiden under the full moon's light. Forever.

The king who ruled then—weak-spined and trembling—agreed without hesitation. What was one life against thousands? A sacred pact was formed, written in strange symbols that squirmed on the parchment. The hungry dragon would be fed, and the rest could live.

Those who later questioned the arrangement learned the folly of defiance. Their sleep became unbearable, filled with crawling horrors. Their waking hours darkened by visions that tore at reason. Within days, the strongest minds fractured. Within a week, most took their own lives.

One man tried to flee beyond the kingdom's borders. Three days later, he returned, crawling on hands and knees. Where his eyes had been were smoking pits. His tongue had been replaced with writhing black centipedes. Before they could silence him, he spoke only once: "There is no escape. It is everywhere."

And so the sacrifices continued. Every full moon, a maiden chosen by lottery. Every full moon, the priests would lead her to the edge of the Blightwood and leave her there with a wreath of black lilies at her feet. Every full moon, she would be gone by morning—no screams, no footprints, no remains. Only occasionally would the people of Silene glimpse the massive silhouette of the beast against the moon, carrying its prey back to whatever foul nest it had made in the mountains beyond the forest.

Tonight marked the thirty-second year of the pact. Tonight, the two-hundred-and-sixty-first maiden would be chosen.

Elias reached the town square where the lottery would be held. Despite the rain—or perhaps because of it—the crowd pressed tight, a sea of hooded figures murmuring prayers. The lottery drum stood on a wooden platform, its bronze surface etched with symbols that matched those of the pact. Inside lay the names of every unmarried woman between sixteen and twenty-five.

The drum began to turn. The crowd fell silent, save for the sound of the rain striking the cobblestones with the rhythm of a fading heartbeat.

Elias closed his eyes. Not his daughter, he prayed to gods he no longer believed in. Not his Lily. Please, not her.

The priest's hand reached into the drum.

Somewhere in the distance, beyond the Blightwood, a thunderous roar split the air. The mountain peaks flashed briefly with fire.

Hungry.

Waiting.

Chapter 1
The Knight Without a Cause

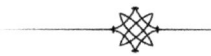

George awakened to the sound of distant thunder, though the sky outside his window hung cloudless, an expanse of deepening blue tinged with the amber of approaching sunset. His body tensed, a soldier's instinct that never truly left. For a moment, he was back on the battlefield—the roar of siege engines, the screams of the dying, the smell of blood and voided bowels.

Then reality reasserted itself. A shabby room in a roadside inn. A hard bed that smelled of must and old straw. The thunder was just a cart passing on the rutted road below.

No—not a cart. The thunder came again, distant but unmistakable. A roar that belonged to no natural creature.

He sat up slowly, mindful of the wound in his side that never fully healed—a parting gift from the final battle before his empire crumbled. The dream clung to him like a shroud, fragments of horror that twisted behind his eyelids.

He saw again the walls of Kastria falling. The imperial standards trampled underfoot. The Emperor's head on a pike. And the fire. Always the fire, consuming everything—wood, stone, flesh— with equal hunger. Fire not from siege weapons, but from the breath of the Emperor's legendary war-dragons, turned against their masters in the final betrayal.

George's hands trembled. He gripped the edge of the bed until his knuckles whitened, focusing on the pain of his fingers digging into the rough wood.

"You died there," he whispered to himself, a daily ritual that kept him tethered to the present. "George the Dragon-Slayer died at Kastria. You're just a man now. Just a man."

He rose stiffly, splashed water on his face from the cracked basin, and dressed. The armor he'd once worn—gleaming plates embossed with the imperial crest—had been sold long ago for traveling coin. Now he wore simple leathers over a tunic of undyed wool. Only his sword remained from his former life, wrapped in oilcloth and hidden beneath the bed. He couldn't bring himself to part with it, though he hadn't drawn it in nearly a year. Its blade had been forged specifically to pierce dragon scales, enchanted by the empire's most powerful mages. With it, he had slain three of the beasts before Kastria fell.

The common room downstairs bustled with more activity than he'd seen during his three-day stay. Men and women spoke in hushed tones, shooting glances at the door as if expecting someone—or something—to burst through at any moment.

The innkeeper, a stout woman with arms thick as oak branches, slid a tankard of ale across the scarred wooden counter.

"Leaving today, traveler?" she asked, though her attention remained on the crowd.

"Perhaps." George took a long drink, savoring the bitterness. "There seems to be some commotion. A festival approaching?"

The woman's laugh was sharp and humorless. "Festival? That's one word for it, I suppose. It's lottery day." She lowered her voice. "The moon grows full tonight."

A chill traced George's spine. He'd heard whispers in his travels, tales of a kingdom in the east where a dragon had taken root. Where sacrifices were made to appease the ancient beast. He'd dismissed them as the kind of stories that flourished in times of hardship—explanations for famine, for plague, for the cruelty of existence.

"This is Silene, then," he said quietly.

The innkeeper's eyes widened slightly. "Aye. Though we don't often name it aloud. Names have power here." She studied him more carefully. "You've heard of us, then? And still you came?"

George shrugged. "I go where the road takes me."

"And what road brings a man with a soldier's eyes and scars to a place even merchants avoid?"

He met her gaze evenly. "A road with no destination."

Something in his tone silenced further questions. The innkeeper nodded once and moved away to serve other patrons.

George finished his ale and stepped outside into the waning daylight. The streets of Silene wound like veins through a diseased body, narrow and convoluted. Buildings leaned toward each other as if sharing secrets, creating alleys where daylight never fully reached. The people moved quickly, eyes down, shoulders hunched. Even the children were quiet, their games subdued versions of what children elsewhere played.

He followed the flow of the crowd toward the town square. Despite himself, curiosity pulled him forward. He had seen many dark things in his years of war—atrocities that haunted his dreams—but never a society built around systematic sacrifice.

The square opened before him, a space paved with stones of such deep gray they appeared almost black. At its center stood a bronze drum atop a wooden platform. Around the drum, twelve robed figures stood in a circle, hoods pulled low. The crowd pressed against the edges of the square but left a wide berth around the platform, as if repelled by an invisible barrier.

The air felt wrong—too thick, too still, charged like the moments before lightning strikes. George instinctively moved his hand to his hip where his sword would have hung, finding only empty air.

A bell tolled somewhere distant, its sound distorted, almost liquid. The hooded figures began to sway. The crowd fell utterly silent.

From the largest building flanking the square—a structure of stone darkened by age and what looked unsettlingly like dried blood—emerged a procession. Guards in tarnished armor escorted a man wearing a crown that seemed too heavy for his thin frame. The King of Silene, George presumed, though he bore little resemblance to any monarch George had served. This king's face was sallow, his eyes sunken, his movements those of a marionette guided by unseen strings.

Behind him walked a young woman dressed in white silk that stood out among the drab colors of the crowd like a star in night sky. Her blond hair cascaded unbound down her back, adorned with small white flowers. Unlike the king, she moved with purpose, her chin raised, her gaze direct.

George found himself unable to look away from her. Not because of her beauty, though she possessed that in abundance, but because of the incongruity she represented—vitality in a place of decay, defiance in a kingdom of submission.

"The Princess," someone murmured nearby. "The King's only child."

The ceremony began. Words spoken in a language George didn't recognize—guttural and slithering. The bronze drum began to turn, seemingly of its own accord. Inside, small wooden tokens clicked against each other like bones.

The King stood slack-jawed and vacant as the drum spun faster, becoming a blur of tarnished metal. The Princess watched with an expression George couldn't decipher—not fear, not resignation, something more complex.

Without warning, the drum stopped. One of the robed figures reached inside and withdrew a single token. The crowd collectively held its breath. The figure passed the token to the King, who stared at it uncomprehendingly.

A whisper ran through the crowd, a sound like dry leaves skittering across stone.

The Princess stepped forward. "Read it, Father," she said, her voice clear and steady.

The King's lips moved silently. Then, in a voice that cracked with disuse: "Selene. Princess Selene of House Blackthorn."

For a heartbeat, silence. Then chaos erupted. People fell to their knees, wailing. Others stood frozen in shock. One of the robed figures collapsed.

The Princess—Selene—showed no surprise. Her expression remained unchanged, as if she had known all along. She simply nodded once and turned to face the crowd.

"The pact will be honored," she called out, her voice cutting through the tumult. "As it has been since the time of my ancestors."

George watched, something stirring within him that he thought had died at Kastria. Not quite outrage, not quite pity—something unnamed that burned in his chest like the beginnings of fever.

The Princess's eyes swept the crowd and, for a moment, met his. Recognition flashed between them, though they had never met—

the recognition of two people standing apart from those around them, observing rather than participating.

Then the guards closed ranks around her, and the procession retreated into the dark building. The crowd began to disperse, moving like sleepwalkers back to their homes to board up windows and doors against the night to come.

George remained in the square long after it emptied, watching as shadows lengthened across the black stones. The air grew colder, carrying a scent like old battlefields—iron and rot and something else, something that made the hair on his arms rise.

"You're not from here," a voice said behind him.

He turned to find one of the robed figures, hood pulled back to reveal the face of an old woman, her skin mapped with lines like dried riverbeds, her eyes milky with cataracts.

"No," George agreed.

"Yet you linger after the choosing." She tilted her head, studying him as if he were a text in an unfamiliar language. "What do you seek in Silene, stranger? We have nothing to offer but sorrow."

"I seek nothing."

"Ah." Her clouded eyes somehow saw too much. "A man running from something, then. From guilt, perhaps? From memory?"

George stiffened. "I'm simply passing through."

"No one simply passes through Silene anymore. The roads lead here by design or don't lead here at all." She stepped closer, the scent of herbs and tallow surrounding her. "I have seen you before, soldier. Not your face, but your kind. Men who carry death like a second skin. Men who have seen too much and now see nothing at all."

His hand clenched into a fist. "What do you want from me, old woman?"

"Want?" She laughed, a sound like stones grinding together. "I want nothing. But the dragon... the dragon may want everything." She reached out a gnarled hand, not quite touching his chest. "There's a spark still alive in you, buried deep beneath the ashes. I wonder if you know it's there."

George stepped back. "Save your riddles. I've no interest in your local superstitions or your sacrificial politics."

"Politics?" The cataract eyes blinked slowly. "You think this is about politics? About power and position?" She shook her head. "You understand nothing. The dragon is real, soldier. As real as the sword you hide, as real as the scars you bear. More real, perhaps."

Another roar echoed across the sky, closer this time. The old woman didn't flinch, but George's eyes darted to the distant mountains where a shadow momentarily blotted out the stars.

She turned to go, then paused. "Tonight, when you sleep—if you sleep—listen for the whispers. They'll tell you what you already know deep in your bones." Her voice dropped to a near-whisper. "Kill the beast, or become it."

Before he could respond, she melded into the gathering darkness, leaving George alone with the echoes of her words and the unsettling feeling that something had just been set in motion that could not be stopped.

That night, as he lay on his hard bed staring at the ceiling, George heard the whispers. They came not from outside but from within, voices that spoke in languages he shouldn't understand but somehow did. They showed him visions—a forest of trees that bled when cut, a temple of black stone where shadows moved independently of light, a dragon coiled around the heart of the world, its scales the color of spilled wine.

And roses. Fields of roses consumed by flame, their petals turning to ash that formed the words: Kill the beast, or become it.

He woke gasping, drenched in sweat, his hand clutching the sword he didn't remember retrieving from beneath the bed.

Outside, the full moon rose over Silene, casting light the color of bone across a land that trembled in anticipation of what the night would bring.

Chapter 2
The Chosen One

Princess Selene Blackthorn stood at her chamber window, watching the moon rise above the twisted spires of Silene. Its light painted the city in shades of silver and ash, transforming familiar buildings into monuments from some forgotten civilization. Beautiful, in its way. Everything looked beautiful from a distance, even dying things.

She didn't turn when the door opened behind her. She recognized her father's shuffling steps, the whisper of his robes across stone.

"Daughter," King Aldric's voice cracked like autumn leaves underfoot. "The priests say... they say there must be some mistake. That your name could not have been in the drum."

"Yet it was." Selene kept her gaze on the moon, now fully visible above the eastern towers. "How strange."

"I've ordered an investigation. The drum will be examined. If someone tampered with the choosing—"

"Who would dare?" She finally turned to face him, taking in his diminished form. Once he had been a powerful man, broad-shouldered and strong-voiced. Now he seemed hollowed out, a husk animated by obligation rather than life. "The pact is sacred. Everyone knows the consequences of interference."

"But you are the princess. The last of our line." His hands trembled as he reached for her, stopping short of actual contact. "You cannot be sacrificed."

Selene felt a flicker of the old anger. Where was this concern when her mother died? When the blight first touched their lands and he retreated into ritual and procedure rather than seeking solutions? When she tried, year after year, to convince him that there must be another way?

"The law applies to all," she said, using the words he had spoken so often. "No exceptions, no exemptions. Isn't that what you taught me?"

"Selene, please..." His eyes, watery and bloodshot, filled with tears. "Let me find a way. There are substitution rituals, binding proxies—"

"No." The word fell between them like a blade. "I will not send another in my place. I will not hide behind privilege while some farmer's daughter dies for me."

King Aldric seemed to age another decade before her eyes. He sank onto a chair, head bowed. "Then I have failed utterly. As a king. As a father."

"You failed long ago," Selene said, not unkindly. "This is merely the culmination."

Outside, a bell tolled—the first of thirteen that would ring throughout the night, marking the hours until dawn. Until the sacrifice.

"I never wanted this life for you," the King whispered. "When you were born, I had such dreams. You would rule justly. You would know peace and prosperity."

"Dreams," Selene echoed. "That's all they ever were."

She moved to her dressing table, fingers tracing the items laid out there—a silver comb passed down through generations of Blackthorn women, a vial of perfume from the southern isles, a dagger with a handle carved from wyvern bone. She picked up the dagger, testing its edge with her thumb.

"Did you know," she said conversationally, "that I've been studying the old texts? The ones locked in the forbidden section of the archives?"

The King's head snapped up. "Those are sealed for a reason. They contain—"

"The truth?" Selene slid the dagger into the sheath hidden in the folds of her dress. "Or at least fragments of it. The dragon wasn't always what it is now. It can be killed."

"Selene, stop. Such knowledge is dangerous. It draws attention we cannot afford."

She laughed, a sound with edges sharp enough to cut. "I'm to be devoured by nightfall. What more attention could I possibly draw?"

The King rose unsteadily. "The sacred texts speak only of sacrifice, not devouring. The maidens become one with the eternal. It is an honor—"

"Spare me the temple propaganda." Selene moved to a chest at the foot of her bed, withdrawing a cloak of midnight blue. "We both know what happens in the Blightwood. The dragon takes them to its lair, and they are never seen again."

Another bell tolled. Twelve hours remaining.

King Aldric reached for her again, this time grasping her arm with surprising strength. "Daughter, listen to me. There are aspects of the pact you don't understand. Things I've shielded you from—"

"I'm not a child anymore." She gently removed his hand. "And I understand more than you know. Why do you think my name was in the drum at all? Why do you think I've prepared for this moment?"

Horror dawned in the King's rheumy eyes. "What have you done?"

Selene smiled, a small, secret expression. "I've done what you never could. I've taken control of my fate."

"The priests will come for you at midnight," he said hoarsely. "They'll lead you to the edge of the Blightwood and leave you there. Alone."

"I know the ritual." She fastened the cloak around her shoulders. "I've watched it every month for years."

The King moved to the door, his shoulders slumped in defeat. "I'll continue searching for alternatives. Perhaps there's still time—"

"Father." Selene's voice softened. "Go to your chambers. Drink your dreamless draught. Sleep through what's to come. That's my final request."

He paused, framed in the doorway like a portrait of failed authority. "I did love you, Selene. In my way."

"I know." She turned back to the window, to the moon now high above the city. "In your way."

After he left, Selene allowed herself a moment of stillness. She had expected to feel fear as the hour approached, but instead found a strange clarity. The path ahead was terrible, yes, but it was a path of her choosing—the first real choice she'd made in a life governed by protocol and expectation.

The third bell tolled. Eleven hours.

A knock at the door, too forceful to be a servant, too hesitant to be a guard.

"Enter," she called, curious.

The door opened to reveal Elias Thorne, the royal historian and her former tutor. His face was gray with worry, his fingers clutching a leather-bound volume.

"My princess," he bowed awkwardly. "Forgive the intrusion."

"Master Thorne." Genuine warmth colored her voice. "You're always welcome."

He stepped inside, closing the door carefully behind him. "I've heard the news. The whole city speaks of nothing else." His eyes, magnified behind thick spectacles, brimmed with uncharacteristic emotion. "It cannot be allowed to happen."

"I'm afraid it must." Selene gestured to a chair. "Unless you've found some loophole in the ancient texts?"

"Not a loophole, exactly." He sat, placing the book on a small table. "But perhaps... an alternative interpretation."

Selene raised an eyebrow. "The priests allow no interpretations beyond their own."

"The priests didn't translate the original pact. I did." Thorne's voice lowered to a conspirator's whisper. "Thirty years ago, when the old tongue was still taught in the academy. Before the temple took control of education."

She leaned forward, intrigued despite herself. "What did you find?"

"The dragon is not invincible. The pact speaks of a weakness—a vulnerability." His fingers trembled as he opened the book to a marked page. "Every beast has its fatal flaw. Even one as ancient as ours."

"And what is the dragon's weakness?"

"Its heart." Thorne turned to another page, where spidery handwriting filled the margins. "The texts speak of a scale missing over its heart—a defect from birth. A single strike there, with the right weapon, could end its reign of terror."

Selene considered this. "Why hasn't this been attempted before?"

"It has." He pointed to notes in the margin. "My predecessor recorded attempts during the early years. They failed. The dragon is not easily approached, and fewer still have weapons that can pierce its hide, even at the vulnerable point."

"And you think I could succeed where others have failed?" Selene touched the dagger hidden in her dress.

"The original pact was sealed by the first Blackthorn king. Your ancestor. His blood runs in your veins." Thorne closed the book reverently. "The dragon might hesitate to strike down a Blackthorn. Just long enough for someone with the right weapon to land a fatal blow."

The fourth bell tolled. Ten hours.

"An interesting theory, Master Thorne." Selene spoke carefully. "But one I cannot test alone. The priests would never permit a deviation from the ritual as they understand it."

"Then we must find help." He leaned closer. "There is a stranger in the city. A man with a sword unlike any I've seen. They say he fought in the eastern wars, for the fallen empire."

The mention sparked something in Selene's memory. "A soldier, by his bearing. I saw him at the choosing ceremony."

The historian nodded eagerly. "The imperial forces were known for their dragon-slayers—elite warriors with enchanted weapons forged specifically to kill the beasts. If this man is one such warrior..."

"Find him," Selene said, making a decision. "Bring him to the royal gardens at dusk. Tell no one."

"But why would he help? What could we offer a man with nothing to lose?"

"Because he has nothing to lose," she said. "And that makes him exactly what we need."

After Thorne left, Selene returned to the window. The city below seemed to hold its breath, streets emptied as people barricaded themselves indoors against the night to come. Beyond the city walls, the Blightwood loomed, a tangled mass of twisted trees and thorny undergrowth that had once been a place of beauty and light.

The fifth bell tolled. Nine hours.

Selene closed her eyes, focusing her thoughts inward. Since childhood, she had experienced dreams unlike others—vivid visions that felt more like memories than fantasies. Dreams of flight over ancient landscapes. Dreams of vast, scaled wings casting shadows over terrified villages. Dreams of hunger so vast it could never be satisfied.

The dragon's dreams, she had come to realize. Somehow, she shared its visions. Felt its desires. Understood its rage.

"I'm coming," she whispered to the presence that always lingered at the edges of her consciousness. "But not as you expect."

Night fell over Silene like a funeral shroud. In the royal gardens, Selene waited by a fountain that no longer flowed, its basin filled with stagnant water the color of old bronze. She had changed from her white ceremonial dress into simpler attire—riding breeches, a fitted tunic, sturdy boots. The cloak concealed her figure, its hood pulled low.

The eighth bell tolled. Six hours.

Footsteps on the gravel path. Two sets—one the familiar shuffling gait of Master Thorne, the other heavier, measured, deliberate.

"Princess," Thorne called softly. "I've brought him, as you asked."

Selene turned to face the stranger properly for the first time. He was tall, broad-shouldered, his face weathered by sun and wind and something deeper—the erosion of the spirit that comes from seeing too much death. A scar bisected his left eyebrow and continued down his cheek, puckered and white against tanned skin. His eyes were the gray of storm clouds, watchful and wary.

"You're the one they call George," she said, not a question.

He inclined his head slightly. "And you're the sacrifice."

Direct. Unadorned by title or protocol. She found it refreshing.

"Not yet," she corrected. "The sacrifice occurs at midnight."

"Why am I here?" He glanced around the garden, taking in exits and potential threats with the practiced ease of a veteran. "Your man was vague about details."

"I have a proposition for you, George of nowhere." Selene gestured for Thorne to leave them. The historian hesitated, then bowed and retreated into the shadows. "One that could benefit us both."

"I doubt that." His hand rested on the hilt of a sword partially concealed beneath his cloak—a warrior's unconscious tell. "I've no interest in court intrigues or doomed heroics."

"Then what do you have interest in?" She stepped closer, studying him. "You came to Silene for a reason. No one comes here by accident anymore."

A muscle twitched in his jaw. "I go where the road leads."

"The road led you here. On the day of the choosing. To witness my selection." She circled him slowly. "Some might call that fate."

"I don't believe in fate." His eyes tracked her movement. "Only consequences."

"Then perhaps you're a consequence I've been waiting for." Selene stopped before him. "I intend to face the dragon tonight. Not as a passive sacrifice, but as a huntress. I need someone who knows how to fight dragons. Someone with nothing to lose."

"You're mad." He said it matter-of-factly. "The beast has devoured hundreds of your people. What chance do you think you have?"

Selene lowered her hood, letting him see her face fully in the moonlight. "The dragon can be killed. I know how."

George's expression didn't change, but something flickered in his eyes—interest, skepticism, perhaps both. "If that were true, it would have been done centuries ago."

"It couldn't have been. The knowledge was lost. Suppressed." She touched her chest, where a pendant lay hidden beneath her tunic. "But I found the truth in ancient texts. The dragon has a weakness—a scale missing over its heart. With the right weapon, at the right moment, it can be slain."

"And you think I have this weapon?"

"Your sword. I recognize the runes etched along its blade. Imperial dragon-slayer steel. Forged to pierce the hide of such beasts."

The ninth bell tolled. Five hours.

George studied her for a long moment. "Even if I believed you—which I don't—why would I help? This isn't my kingdom. These aren't my people. Their troubles are their own."

"Because you dream of fire," she said softly. "Because you hear whispers even when awake. Because something inside you recognized something inside me the moment our eyes met in the square."

He took a step back, his hand tightening on his sword hilt. "What are you?"

"The same as you. A pawn that refused to stay in place." Selene held his gaze. "The dragon's influence extends far beyond Silene now. It grows stronger with each sacrifice. Soon, no kingdom will be beyond its reach. No mind safe from its corruption."

"You know a great deal for someone who's never left the palace."

"I know what it shows me," she said simply. "As it shows you."

George fell silent, conflict evident in the tension of his shoulders, the tightness around his eyes. Finally, he spoke. "What exactly do you propose?"

"When the priests leave me at the edge of the forest at midnight, I'll begin my journey to the dragon's lair in the mountains beyond. You will follow, keeping enough distance that they don't detect you." Selene outlined her plan with the precision of someone who had contemplated it many times. "Together, we'll confront the beast. Strike at its heart. End this."

"And if we fail?"

"Then I die as intended, and you can return to your aimless wandering with a clear conscience." Her smile held no humor. "Nothing ventured, nothing gained."

The tenth bell tolled. Four hours.

George unsheathed his sword partly, examining the blade in the moonlight. Ancient runes etched along its length caught the silver glow, seeming to pulse with inner light.

"Imperial steel," he said quietly. "Forged in dragon fire, then quenched in dragon blood. One of the few possessions I kept after Kastria fell." He resheathed it with a decisive movement. "It has tasted the blood of three of these beasts. Perhaps it's time it claimed a fourth."

Selene felt something unfamiliar stir within her—hope, fragile as a butterfly's wing. "Then you'll help me?"

"I'll follow you into the forest," he conceded. "Beyond that, we'll see what fate—or consequence—has in store."

She extended her hand. After a moment's hesitation, he clasped it. His palm was calloused, warm against her cool skin. The contact sent a jolt through her, a sensation like recognition.

In that moment, something shifted between them—a covenant formed without words, sealed by touch and the shared knowledge of dreams darker than night.

The eleventh bell tolled. Three hours until midnight. Three hours until Princess Selene of House Blackthorn entered the Blightwood, not as a sacrifice, but as a huntress.

And she would not go alone.

Chapter 3
The Hunter's Path

The procession moved through streets emptied by fear, torches casting long shadows that danced like specters across boarded windows and barred doors. Twelve priests in formal regalia surrounded Princess Selene, their monotonous chanting rising and falling like the breath of some great beast. Behind them walked King Aldric, supported by two guards, his face slack with the effects of whatever draught he had consumed to dull his awareness of the night's events.

George watched from the shadows of an alleyway, his hand resting on his sword hilt. He had shed his traveler's cloak for darker attire that would serve him better in the night—a hunter's leathers acquired through means best not examined too closely. A pack containing basic supplies rested against his back: water, dried meat, flint and steel, bandages. Provisions for a journey he didn't expect to survive.

The princess walked with her head high, refusing the blindfold traditionally offered to sacrifices. Her midnight-blue cloak billowed behind her in the chill wind that always preceded dawn in this blighted land. If she felt fear, it didn't show in her measured stride or composed features.

The procession reached the northern gate—a massive structure of ironwood and black iron. The metal bands crossing the wooden beams were etched with the same strange symbols George had seen on the bronze drum, patterns that hurt the eye if observed too long. The guards stationed there averted their gaze as the priests approached, making signs of warding across their chests.

"Open for the sacred offering," intoned the lead priest, his voice distorted, as if speaking through water.

The gates groaned inward. Beyond them stretched a barren tract of land—no-man's-land, a buffer between civilization and corruption. And beyond that, the Blightwood waited, a wall of twisted trees whose branches seemed to reach toward the procession with arthritic fingers.

In the distance, a howl rose—not wolf, not human, something that existed in the uneasy territory between. The priests faltered momentarily, their chanting interrupted before resuming with forced conviction.

The procession stopped at the edge of the no-man's-land. Here, a stone altar stood—a simple rectangular block stained dark by the blood of countless rituals. Flanking the altar were two stone pillars, each topped with a brazier that burned with unnatural green flame.

Selene was led to the altar. The priests arranged themselves in a circle around her, their robes rippling in the unnatural stillness of the air.

"Maiden of Silene," the high priest began, his voice carrying unnaturally in the quiet. "Child of the sacred bloodline. You stand at the threshold of transformation. Through your sacrifice, the many are preserved. Through your offering, the covenant remains unbroken."

Selene said nothing, her gaze fixed on the forest beyond.

"Do you come willingly to fulfill the pact of your ancestors?" the priest asked.

"I come willingly," she replied, her voice clear and unwavering. "To fulfill a purpose centuries in the making."

The priest hesitated, something in her tone giving him pause, but continued with the ritual. "Then receive the mark of the chosen."

He dipped his thumb in a vial of dark liquid and pressed it to Selene's forehead. The substance sizzled against her skin, leaving a symbol that glowed briefly before fading to a dull red—a stylized eye within a spiral.

"At the witching hour, you will walk the path alone," the priest instructed. "Neither turning back nor straying from the way. What waits beyond is your destiny. What lies behind is no longer your concern."

The priests withdrew, forming two lines that extended back toward the gate. One by one, they extinguished their torches in vessels of dark sand, plunging the area into deeper darkness. Only the green flames of the braziers remained, casting a sickly glow over the scene.

The high priest was the last to retreat. He paused, studying Selene with an unreadable expression.

"The Blackthorn line ends tonight," he said, his voice low enough that only she could hear. "Perhaps it is fitting. Perhaps it was always meant to be."

Selene smiled thinly. "Nothing ends tonight, High Priest. But something begins."

He stepped back, troubled by her response. "May your passage be swift," he said, the traditional farewell to the sacrificed.

"Oh, it will be anything but swift," she replied.

The priests withdrew through the gate, which closed behind them with a sound like a tomb being sealed. Only King Aldric remained, supported by his guards, swaying slightly as he struggled to focus on his daughter's distant figure.

"Take me back," he slurred to the guards. "I cannot watch."

As they helped the broken king return to his castle, George emerged from his hiding place among the ruins that dotted the no-man's-land. He moved silently toward the altar where Selene waited, keeping to the shadows until he reached her.

"They're gone," he said quietly.

She nodded, not turning. "Good. Now we must move quickly. The dragon is already restless—can you feel it?"

In the distance, the mountains silhouetted against the night sky seemed to shift, as though something massive was moving upon them. A low rumble, like distant thunder but deeper, more guttural, rolled across the land.

George drew his sword, the runes along its length glowing with a blue-white light that cut through the darkness. "Which way?"

"Through the Blightwood. There's a path known only to the royal bloodline—a quicker route to the mountains than the common roads." She touched the mark on her forehead, which had begun to pulse faintly. "This will guide us."

They crossed the no-man's-land quickly, the withered grass crunching beneath their boots. As they approached the forest's edge, the air grew thick, resistant, as if the boundary between Silene and the Blightwood was more than just physical space.

Selene paused at the threshold, taking a deep breath. Then, with determination etched in every line of her body, she stepped onto a barely visible trail. George followed, suppressing a shudder as the forest seemed to close around them like a fist.

The path twisted immediately, turning in ways that defied natural geometry. Trees that appeared distant from outside now loomed overhead, their branches forming a canopy so dense that moonlight penetrated only in thin, silver needles. The air smelled of decay and something else—something metallic and ancient.

"Keep to the center of the path," Selene warned. "The forest feeds on those who stray."

As if to emphasize her point, a rustling sound came from the undergrowth beside them. George glimpsed movement—a shape that might have once been a deer but was now a grotesque parody, its limbs elongated and jointed in impossible ways, antlers spiraling like corkscrews into what remained of its skull. It watched them with eyes that glowed with the same sickly green as the braziers, then melted back into the shadows.

"The dragon's corruption transforms everything it touches," Selene explained, noticing his disturbed expression. "Plants, animals, people. Nothing remains as it was."

They continued in silence, following the twisting path deeper into the forest. The trees grew stranger the further they went—some with bark that pulsed like living flesh, others weeping a thick, dark substance from knots that resembled screaming mouths. Fungi of impossible colors sprouted from fallen trunks, emitting spores that danced in the air like malevolent fireflies.

Time lost meaning in the Blightwood. What felt like hours might have been minutes; what seemed momentary could have been an eternity. The only constant was the path before them and the sense of being watched by countless unseen eyes.

George kept his sword ready, its glow providing both illumination and a degree of protection. Twice they were accosted by creatures that defied description—amalgamations of wildlife twisted by the dragon's influence—and twice his blade dispatched them with clean efficiency.

Suddenly, the trees thinned, and they emerged onto the slope of a mountain. Above them, the night sky opened up, stars glittering like scattered diamonds across a canvas of deepest black. The air here was clearer, colder, edged with the scent of stone and snow.

"We've cleared the forest," George observed, surprised. "I didn't expect our passage to be so—"

A roar split the night, so powerful it shook loose stones from the mountainside. They clattered past, narrowly missing the pair as they pressed themselves against the rock face.

"He knows we're here," Selene whispered, her eyes wide. "He's been waiting."

They climbed steadily, following a path that wound up the mountainside. As they ascended, George noticed ancient carvings in the stone walls—symbols similar to those on the bronze drum, but older, more primal. The path itself grew more obviously constructed, with steps cut directly into the rock at steeper sections.

"This wasn't made by the dragon," George said, running his hand along a perfectly straight section of wall.

"No. These are remnants of the original temple—the one built by my ancestors when they first sealed the pact with the dragon." Selene's voice was tight with controlled emotion. "Before it betrayed them and took the mountain for itself."

The path ended at a massive stone platform jutting out from the mountainside. Before them gaped the entrance to a cave, its mouth a perfect arch that could never have been formed by natural processes. Within, darkness waited, absolute and hungry.

"The dragon's lair," Selene said unnecessarily. "Beyond lies a cavern large enough to house a beast the size of a small castle."

George gripped his sword tighter, its runes flaring in response to his resolve. "How do we proceed? I doubt we can simply walk in and catch it napping."

"We don't need to." Selene withdrew a small object from within her tunic—a pendant of dark metal inscribed with symbols that matched those on the cave entrance. "This belonged to my mother. It contains the blood of the first Blackthorn king. With it, I can summon the dragon."

"Summon it? Here, in the open?" George looked around the exposed platform. "We'll be completely vulnerable."

"Not completely." She pointed to a series of stone columns ringing the platform, each carved with runes similar to those on his sword. "These were placed here by the original dragon-slayers, centuries ago. They limit the dragon's power, prevent it from using its full magic against us."

"That still leaves its teeth, claws, and fire," George noted dryly.

"Which is why I have you." Selene smiled grimly. "A man who has slain three such beasts."

Before he could respond, she stepped to the center of the platform and held the pendant aloft. It caught the moonlight, seeming to absorb and amplify it until it glowed with an inner radiance.

"Hear me, Ancient One," she called, her voice carrying a strange harmonic quality. "I, Selene of House Blackthorn, invoke the pact of blood and bone. I offer myself as sacrifice, as is the custom. Come forth and claim what is yours by ancient right."

For a moment, nothing happened. Then, a tremor ran through the mountain, causing dust and small stones to cascade down from the heights above. A deeper rumble followed, and with it, the sound of something massive moving within the cave.

George positioned himself beside Selene, sword at the ready. "When it emerges, stay behind me. Wait for my signal before attempting anything."

She nodded, slipping the pendant back around her neck and drawing the wyvern-bone dagger from its sheath. "Remember, aim for the missing scale over its heart. You'll know it when you see it—a darker patch on the left side of its chest."

A gust of hot, foul wind erupted from the cave mouth, carrying with it the stench of carrion and sulfur. Then came a sound—a rhythmic thumping that George recognized immediately as the footfalls of something impossibly large.

"Steady," he murmured, more to himself than to Selene.

The darkness within the cave mouth shifted, coalesced, and suddenly erupted outward as the dragon emerged.

It was massive beyond comprehension—easily sixty feet from snout to tail-tip, with a wingspan twice that when partially unfurled. Its scales were the deep crimson of old blood, edged with black that seemed to absorb light rather than reflect it. The head alone was the size of a wagon, crowned with horns that curved back like a grotesque parody of a royal diadem. Eyes the size of dinner plates glowed amber in the moonlight, vertical pupils contracting as they focused on the two humans daring to stand before it.

"Blackthorn," the dragon rumbled, its voice like the movement of tectonic plates. "You come willingly, as is proper. But you bring... a champion?" It swung its massive head toward George, nostrils flaring. "I smell imperial steel. I smell the blood of my kindred on your blade, slayer."

George said nothing, measuring the distance between himself and the beast, noting the placement of its limbs, the angle of its wings. He had faced dragons before, but never one so ancient, so massive. The creatures bred for the imperial armies had been a fraction of this beast's size.

"I come with a champion, yes," Selene replied, her voice steady despite standing before a creature that could devour her in a single bite. "But not for the reason you think."

The dragon's laugh was like an avalanche, rocks tumbling down a mountainside. "Your reasons matter not, little princess. The pact remains. Your blood belongs to me, as did the blood of all those maidens before you." It lowered its head until its eye was level with Selene. "Though I admit, royal blood makes for a sweeter feast."

"The pact was built on lies," Selene said boldly. "My ancestors summoned you for power, and you betrayed them. Turned their own magic against them."

"Betrayal?" The dragon reared back, affronted. "I gave them exactly what they asked for—power beyond mortal means. Is it my fault they did not anticipate the cost?" Its massive tail swept across the platform, forcing George and Selene to dive in opposite directions to avoid being crushed.

"Enough talk," George called, regaining his footing. "Face me, beast. Or are you only brave enough to devour maidens who cannot fight back?"

The dragon's head swiveled toward him, eyes narrowing. "You think yourself a dragon-slayer, little man? The runts you faced in the imperial wars were pale shadows of my majesty." It inhaled deeply, chest expanding. "Let us see how imperial steel fares against true dragon fire."

George dove behind one of the stone columns as the dragon exhaled a torrent of flame so hot it turned the rock molten where it struck. The column groaned but held, its protective runes flaring blue-white against the onslaught.

"The columns," Selene shouted from her position behind another pillar. "They absorb the dragon's fire. Use them for cover, move between them!"

George nodded, already formulating a strategy. "Keep it distracted," he called back. "I need to get closer to its chest."

Selene stepped out from behind her column, pendant held high. "Dragon!" she shouted. "You've broken faith with the Blackthorn line. I reclaim what my ancestors gave!"

The dragon's attention snapped to her, its massive body pivoting with surprising grace for something so large. "Reclaim? Foolish girl. Your ancestors gave me dominion over this land in perpetuity. You cannot undo what has been done."

As it focused on Selene, George darted from his position, using the columns for cover, moving steadily closer to the dragon's left flank. The beast was so intent on Selene that it didn't notice his approach until he was nearly upon it.

With a warrior's cry, George lunged from behind the final column, sword aimed at the darker patch of scales Selene had described. But the dragon was faster than he anticipated—its tail whipped around, catching him mid-stride and sending him tumbling across the platform.

He rolled to his feet, breath knocked from his lungs but otherwise unharmed. His sword, still firmly in his grip, flared brighter as if responding to the threat.

"Predictable," the dragon rumbled. "Like all your kind, you think straightforward violence is the answer." It stalked toward him, claws scoring deep gouges in the stone platform. "I've lived for millennia, slayer. I've faced weapons far more formidable than yours."

George steadied himself, sword at the ready. "Yet still you hide in your cave, feeding on helpless sacrifices rather than facing warriors who can hurt you."

The dragon's rage was palpable, the temperature around them rising as fire built in its chest. "I hide from NOTHING!"

It lunged forward with shocking speed, jaws open wide to engulf George whole. He dived to the side, rolling under the dragon's outstretched neck and coming up beneath its chest. There, exposed for just a moment, he saw it—a patch of darker scales, and in the center, a gap where one scale was missing entirely, revealing vulnerable flesh beneath.

Without hesitation, George thrust upward with all his strength, the enchanted blade sinking deep into the dragon's flesh.

The beast's roar of pain shook the very mountain, sending cascades of rock tumbling down from the heights above. It reared back, tearing the sword from George's grip as it remained embedded in the wound.

"BETRAYAL!" it bellowed, fire spewing from its maw in an uncontrolled conflagration that scorched the platform and set nearby trees aflame. "YOU DARE!"

George scrambled backward, now weaponless, as the dragon thrashed in agony. Blood as dark as wine poured from the wound, steaming where it struck the stone. But to his dismay, the sword hadn't reached deep enough—the dragon was injured, but far from slain.

Selene appeared at his side, pulling him behind a column as another gout of flame swept the platform. "The sword," she gasped. "It's still in its chest."

"Not deep enough," George replied grimly. "I couldn't get a clean angle."

The dragon was now in a frenzy of pain and rage, its massive body slamming against the mountain, causing tremors that threatened to collapse the entire platform. Its tail whipped back and forth, destroying columns with each pass. Fire erupted from its mouth in uncontrolled bursts, turning the night to day.

"We need to finish it," Selene said, determination in her eyes. "One more strike to drive the sword home."

"How? I can't get close again without being incinerated."

Selene touched the pendant at her throat. "There's another way." She turned to him, a decision forming in her eyes. "The old texts spoke of more than just the dragon's weakness. They spoke of a bond between the Blackthorn line and the beast—a connection of blood and magic."

"What are you suggesting?"

"The pendant—it doesn't just contain my ancestor's blood. It contains a fragment of his soul, bound to the dragon through the original pact." She gripped it tightly. "With it, I can momentarily subdue the beast. Freeze it in place. But only for seconds."

George understood immediately. "Long enough for me to reach the sword and drive it home."

She nodded, her expression solemn. "But there's a cost. Using the pendant this way... it will bind me to the dragon's fate."

The implications struck him like a physical blow. "You mean—"

"If the dragon dies, I die." She smiled sadly. "A true sacrifice, after all."

"No," George gripped her arm. "There has to be another way."

40

"There isn't." Another column exploded as the dragon's tail struck it. "This is what I was born for, George. This is why my name was in the drum." She pressed something into his hand—a small, ornate key. "When it's done, return to Silene. In the royal library, behind the painting of the first king, there's a hidden compartment. Inside is a book detailing how to cleanse the land of the dragon's corruption."

Before he could protest further, she darted out from behind the column, pendant held high. "DRAGON!" she shouted. "HEAR ME!"

The beast's head swung toward her, its frenzy momentarily checked by her audacity.

"By the blood of the first Blackthorn, by the magic of the ancient pact, I bind you!" She pressed the pendant to her lips, then hurled it directly at the dragon's face.

The pendant struck the beast between its eyes and shattered in a burst of blinding light. The dragon froze in mid-motion, every muscle locked, eyes wide with shock and fury. A keening wail emerged from its throat, but it could not move, could not unleash its fire.

"NOW!" Selene screamed, her body rigid, blood streaming from her nose and eyes as she maintained the magical connection.

George didn't hesitate. He sprinted across the platform, leapt onto the dragon's foreleg, and scrambled up its massive shoulder. The beast trembled beneath him, fighting the magical constraint with every fiber of its being.

Reaching the protruding hilt of his sword, George grasped it with both hands and threw his entire weight behind it, driving the blade deeper into the dragon's heart.

The enchanted steel slid home with a sound like thunder. The dragon's body convulsed, a spasm so violent it threw George clear. He landed hard on the platform, rolling to the edge where only a desperate grab prevented him from plummeting down the mountainside.

A sound unlike anything he'd ever heard tore through the night—part roar, part scream, a death cry that contained within it centuries of rage and pain. The dragon reared up to its full height, wings extended, fire erupting from its mouth, eyes, and wound. Its body began to glow from within, as if its own fire was consuming it from the inside out.

And in that moment of the dragon's death, Selene collapsed to the ground, her body arching in perfect synchrony with the beast's final spasm.

"SELENE!" George crawled toward her, battered and exhausted but driven by desperate need.

The dragon's massive body began to disintegrate, scales falling away like autumn leaves, flesh crumbling to ash, bone turning to dust. As it collapsed, a shockwave of energy burst outward from its heart, washing over the platform, the mountain, the forest below.

Where the wave passed, corruption receded. Twisted trees straightened. Sickly green light faded. The very air seemed to clear, as if a miasma centuries old had finally dissipated.

George reached Selene's side, gathering her limp form in his arms. Her skin was cold, her eyes closed, blood drying on her pale face.

"No," he whispered, cradling her head. "Not like this. Not when we've won."

Around them, the mountain continued to transform as the dragon's death released the land from its corrupting influence. Dawn broke over the horizon, the first natural sunrise Silene had seen in generations—clean light, unsullied by the dragon's malevolence.

In his arms, Selene remained still, her sacrifice complete.

Until, impossibly, she stirred.

Her eyes fluttered open, no longer the blue they had been, but a strange, luminous amber—the color of the dragon's eyes, but without the malice that had burned there.

"George," she whispered, her voice carrying an otherworldly resonance. "You did it."

"We did it," he corrected, joy and confusion warring within him. "But how—I thought the binding meant you would die with it?"

She smiled weakly. "The binding meant our fates were joined. But it seems the dragon had more to offer in death than in life." She raised a trembling hand to touch his face. "Its power—not its corruption, but its true magic—needed somewhere to go. The pendant... it directed that power into me."

As the sun rose fully above the horizon, bathing them in golden light, George helped Selene to her feet. Together, they stood on the transformed mountain, looking out over a land already beginning to heal.

In the distance, the spires of Silene gleamed not with sickly green light, but with the natural reflection of the morning sun. The Blightwood below was transforming before their eyes, corruption receding like an outgoing tide, leaving healthy forest in its wake.

"What happens now?" George asked, his arm supporting her still-weak form.

Selene looked down at her hands, where faint patterns like scales shimmered beneath her skin when caught in direct sunlight. "Now we rebuild. We heal the land completely. We ensure no one ever again makes pacts with powers they don't understand."

She turned to him, her dragon-amber eyes meeting his. "That is, if you're willing to stay. Silene will need a protector while it recovers. Someone who understands the dangers of power misused."

George thought of the road that had led him here, of the aimless wandering that had followed Kastria's fall. Of the purpose he had thought forever lost.

He smiled, taking her hand in his. "I think my wandering days are over, Princess. It seems I've found a cause worth fighting for after all."

Epilogue
The River of Stars

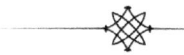

One year later, George stood on the balcony of the royal palace, watching as dawn broke over a Silene transformed. The city gleamed in the morning light, rebuilt and renewed. Where once twisted spires had scraped a sickly sky, now elegant towers reached toward clear blue heavens. The fields beyond the walls rippled with golden grain, and the orchards bent low with the weight of their bounty.

The Blightwood was no more—in its place grew a healthy forest, wildlife returning to lands long abandoned. The people of Silene walked with heads held high, the shadow of centuries lifted from their shoulders.

As Captain of the Royal Guard and personal protector to the Queen, George had overseen much of the transformation. His experience fighting dragons had proven invaluable as they hunted down the last vestiges of corruption—smaller beasts born of the great dragon's influence, hiding in remote corners of the kingdom.

The sword that had slain the beast now hung above the throne, a reminder of both victory and sacrifice. Its runes no longer glowed with battle-magic, but it remained a symbol of a new era.

Behind him, the door to the balcony opened. He turned to see Selene, resplendent in a gown of midnight blue embroidered with silver stars—the new colors of House Blackthorn, chosen to represent the night sky cleansed of corruption.

"You're up early," she said, joining him at the railing.

"Old habits," he replied with a smile. "A soldier rises with the sun."

She leaned against him, her warmth welcome in the cool morning air. The scales that sometimes shimmered beneath her skin caught the sunlight, iridescent patterns that reminded them both of the power that now flowed through her veins—the dragon's magic, purified by her sacrifice and transformed into something that healed rather than corrupted.

"The delegation from the Eastern Kingdoms arrives today," she said. "They're eager to establish trade now that the roads to Silene are safe again."

"And to see the Dragon Queen for themselves, I imagine." George tucked a strand of her hair behind her ear. "Tales of your transformation have spread far and wide."

She laughed softly. "Is that what they're calling me? How dramatic."

"Would you prefer 'The Queen Who Lived'? Or perhaps 'Selene Dragonheart'?"

"I would prefer just Selene," she said, though her smile took any sting from the words. "Though I suppose some titles are inevitable when one absorbs the power of an ancient dragon."

They stood in comfortable silence, watching the city awaken below them. Children played in streets once too dangerous to walk. Merchants set up stalls in squares that had previously hosted only grim ceremonies. Life had returned to Silene in all its beautiful chaos.

"Do you ever regret it?" George asked suddenly. "Binding yourself to the dragon's fate, not knowing what would happen?"

Selene considered the question, her amber eyes—the most visible reminder of her transformation—gazing into the distance. "No," she said finally. "Even if the outcome had been different, it was a choice freely made. After a lifetime of having choices made for me, that alone would have been worth it."

She turned to face him, taking both his hands in hers. "And you? Do you regret following a strange princess into battle against a dragon that wasn't yours to fight?"

George thought of the aimless wanderer he had been, haunted by failure and loss. The man who had died at Kastria, reborn in the crucible of Silene's liberation.

"Never," he said, pulling her close. "It was the only path worth taking."

As the sun rose fully over the renewed kingdom, Queen Selene and her champion stood together on the balcony, guardians of a land reborn from sacrifice and courage, their fates entwined like the river of stars above.

The end was just the beginning.

THE END

Enjoyed this book?

Share your thoughts with a review and help more readers discover it! Your feedback truly makes a difference.

☆ ☆ ☆ ☆ ☆

To be the first to read my next book or for any suggestions about new translations, visit: https://arielsandersbooks.com/

SPECIAL BONUS

Want this Bonus Ebook for *free*?

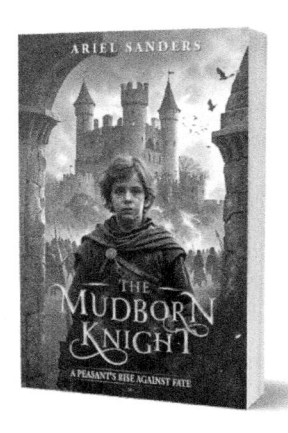

SCAN W/ YOUR CAMERA TO DOWNLOAD THE EBOOK!

Printed in Dunstable, United Kingdom